The star in the Christmas play
E Lyn   39092001061029

Silver City Public Library

D0118623

The Star in the Christmas Play

Written by
LYNNE MARIE

Illustrated by
LORNA HUSSEY

beaming books
MINNEAPOLIS

SILVER CITY PUBLIC LIBRARY
515 W. COLLEGE AVE.
SILVER CITY, NM 88061

0279249

E
Lyn
$17.00
12/18

Text copyright © 2018 Lynne Marie

Illustrations copyright © 2018 Lorna Hussey

Published in 2018 by Beaming Books, an imprint of 1517 Media. All rights reserved. No part of this book may be reproduced without the written permission of the publisher. Email copyright@1517.media. Printed in the United States of America.

First edition published 2018
24 23 22 21 20 19 18   1 2 3 4 5 6 7 8

ISBN: 9781506438139

Design by Alison Stuerman, Mighty Media, Inc.
Production by Tory Herman, 1517 Media

Library of Congress Cataloging-in-Publication Data

Names: Lynne Marie, author. | Hussey, Lorna, illustrator.
Title: The star in the Christmas play / written by Lynne Marie ; illustrated
  by Lorna Hussey.
Description: First edition. | Minneapolis : Beaming Books, 2018. | Summary:
  All of the savannah animals are excited to audition for the school
  Christmas play, except Raffi the giraffe, who feels discouraged about
  being extremely tall, until he realizes that that he is just the right
  size to play the most important part.
Identifiers: LCCN 2018028196 | ISBN 9781506438139 (hardcover : alk. paper)
Subjects: LCSH: Jesus Christ--Nativity--Juvenile fiction. | CYAC: Jesus
  Christ--Nativity--Fiction. | Christmas--Fiction. | Size--Fiction. |
  Self-acceptance--Fiction. | Theater--Fiction. | Giraffe--Fiction. |
  Grassland animals--Fiction.
Classification: LCC PZ7.L99526 St 2018 | DDC [E]--dc23 LC record available at https://lccn.loc.gov/2018028196

VN0004589; 9781506438139; SEPT2018

Beaming Books
510 Marquette Avenue
Minneapolis, MN 55402
beamingbooks.com

"I wish I were any animal but a giraffe," said Raffi. Instead of running toward savanna school like usual, he dragged his hooves.

Mother nuzzled his neck.
"What's wrong, little one?"

"I'm big. A giant! I'll never get
a part in the Christmas play."

Mother smiled. "You're just the right size."
Raffi sighed. "I'm not the right size at all!"
"Someday," said Mother, "you'll
appreciate how tall you are."

When Raffi arrived at school, he joined the others in the audition line. "I'm trying out for baby Jesus," said Lion Cub. He curled into a little ball. "I'd love to be Mary!" Meerkat practiced looking meek.

"I hope to be Joseph," said Cheetah, using a deep voice.
"I'm a shoe-in for the camel!" Camel arched his back.
"With a little fleece, I'd make a swell sheep," said Baby Hippo.

Everyone giggled, except Raffi.

Someone as tall as I am could never be a star. He slumped.

Mrs. Ostrich began the tryouts. Each animal acted out a scene. When Raffi's turn came, he read Joseph's part.

Everyone applauded.
"Well done," said Mrs. Ostrich.

That afternoon, Raffi raced home. "I read so well, Mama. Everyone clapped. Maybe someone as tall as I am can be a star."

Mother smiled.
"You're my star."

The next day, Raffi galloped so fast to school, he even beat Cheetah there. He couldn't wait to hear which part Mrs. Ostrich assigned to whom.

One by one, Mrs. Ostrich read out the parts. Lion would play baby Jesus.

Meerkat would be Mary, and Cheetah, Joseph. Gnu and Camel both got to play camels.

Raffi's lips twitched.
Will I even get a part at all?

Someone as tall as I am could never be a star. He slouched.

All, from the aardvarks to the hyenas, hooted and howled with joy as they received their parts...

except Raffi, who wanted to kick up dirt and run home.

Then, Mrs. Ostrich called his name. "Raffi, I've not yet assigned your role..." she began. Raffi bent down and whispered to her. "I'm too tall, aren't I?"
"Yes."

"I can't play a lead role, because I don't fit in the manger."
"Yes."

"I can't play a manger animal, because I'll block the others from view."
"Yes."

"I can't play an angel, as
I'll fall through the roof."
She nodded.

"But don't worry," said Mrs. Ostrich, "I'm sure we'll come up with something." She patted his long neck and paused...

Raffi looked longingly
at the stage and then
up, up, up at the sky. He
remembered his mother
told him, *You're my star*.

Then, a thought came to him.
He whispered in Mrs. Ostrich's ear.

"What a fine idea," she said.
"That's truly an important part!"

On Christmas Eve, all the savanna babies took their places behind the curtain. Except Raffi, who hid behind the manger.

The Nativity play began...

When the babe was born,
a bright light rose above the manger.

By the light of this guiding star, the wise men
and shepherds found their way to the baby Jesus.

Raffi beamed.
After all, he was
the star in the
Christmas play.